Fall Animal Fun

Martha E. H. Rustad

Illustrated by Amanda Enright

LERNER PUBLICATIONS ◆ MINNEAPOLIS

NOTE TO EDUCATORS

Find text recall questions at the end of each chapter. Critical-thinking and text feature questions are available on page 23. These help young readers learn to think critically about the topic by using the text, text features, and illustrations.

Lerner Publications Company
A division of Lerner Publishing Group, Inc.
241 First Avenue North
Minneapolis, MN 55401 USA

For reading levels and more information, look up this title at www.lernerbooks.com.

Photos on p. 22 used with permission of: Ricardo Reitmeyer/Shutterstock.com (deer); Geoffrey Kuchera/Shutterstock.com (bear); JHVEPhoto/Shutterstock.com (butterflies).

Main body text set in Billy Infant 22/28.
Typeface provided by SparkyType.

Library of Congress Cataloging-in-Publication Data

Names: Rustad, Martha E. H. (Martha Elizabeth Hillman), 1975- author. | Enright, Amanda, illustrator.
Title: Fall animal fun / Martha E. H. Rustad ; illustrated by Amanda Enright.
Description: Minneapolis : Lerner Publications, [2018] | Series: Fall fun (Early bird stories) | Includes bibliographical references and index.
Identifiers: LCCN 2017058245 (print) | LCCN 2017049721 (ebook) | ISBN 9781541524903 (eb pdf) | ISBN 9781541520004 (lb : alk. paper) | ISBN 9781541527171 (pb : alk. paper)
Subjects: LCSH: Animal behavior—Juvenile literature. | Adaptation (Biology)—Juvenile literature. | Autumn—Juvenile literature.
Classification: LCC QL751.5 (print) | LCC QL751.5 .R88225 2018 (ebook) | DDC 578.4/3—dc23

LC record available at https://lccn.loc.gov/2017058245

Manufactured in the United States of America
1-44336-34582-12/11/2017

TABLE OF CONTENTS

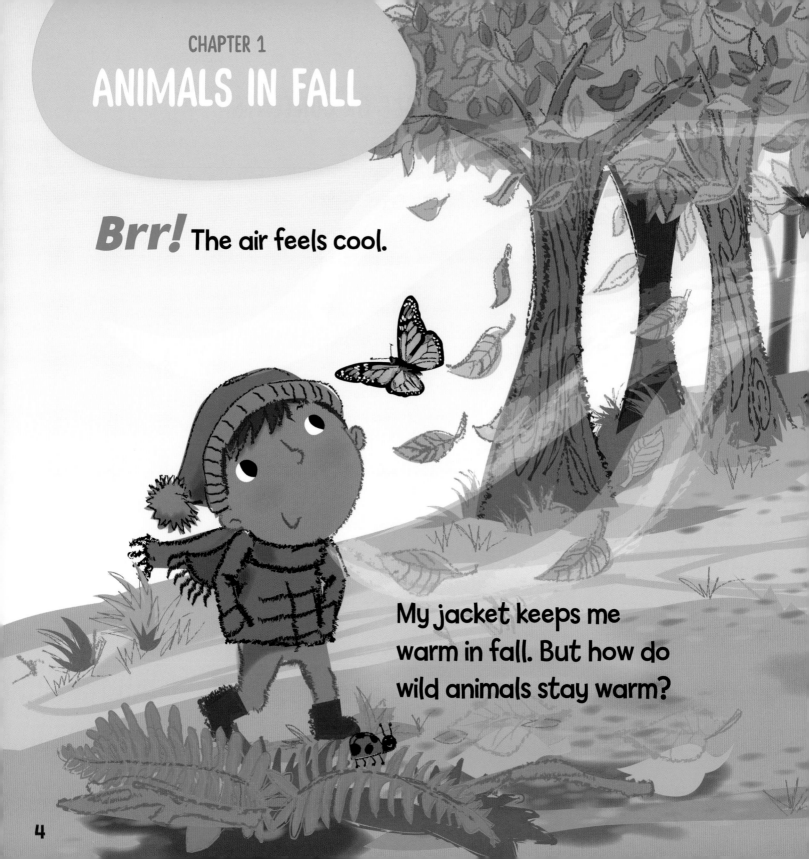

CHAPTER 1
ANIMALS IN FALL

Brr! The air feels cool.

My jacket keeps me warm in fall. But how do wild animals stay warm?

In fall, animals get ready for winter. Some animals go south. Some go to sleep. And some change.

What do animals do in fall?

CHAPTER 2
SOME ANIMALS GO SOUTH

Whoosh! Gray whales swim by.

In fall, gray whales swim from
Alaska to Mexico.

Flutter! Monarch butterflies fly south in fall.

They fly all morning.

They eat in the afternoon.

They rest at night.
They cannot live in cold weather.
It is warmer in the South.

Honk! Canada geese fly across the sky. They form a V-shape.

Canada geese migrate south.

Why do animals go south in fall?

CHAPTER 3
SOME ANIMALS SLEEP

Grr! Black bears look for a small den in the fall.

They will sleep in the
den when winter comes.

Ssss! Rattlesnakes slither to their dens in fall.

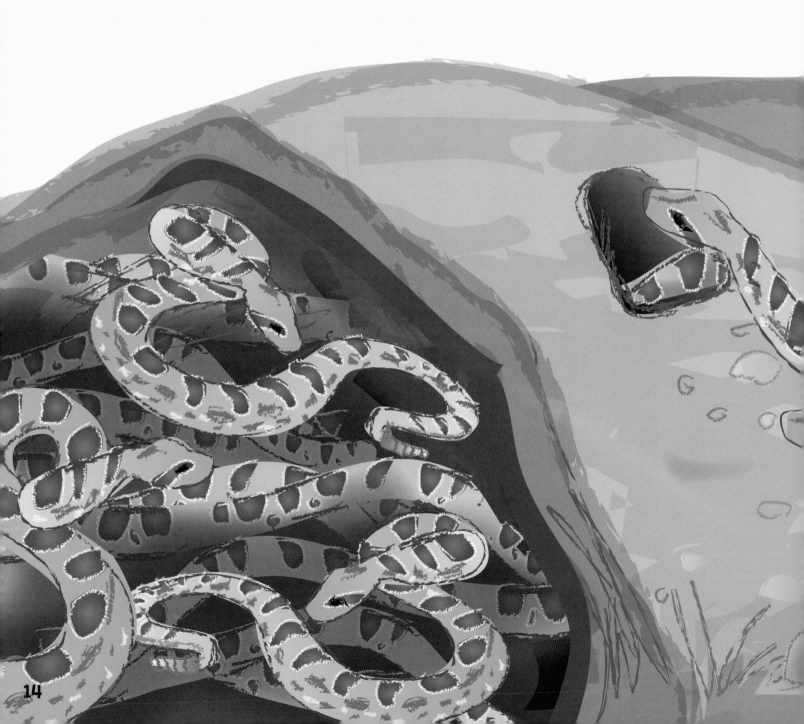

They hibernate in caves or holes in the ground that will not freeze.

Why do snakes and bears find dens in fall?

CHAPTER 4

SOME ANIMALS CHANGE

Hop! Snowshoe hares change color in fall.

In winter, they must be white to match the snow.

This color protects them from animals that might eat them.

Munch! White-tailed deer eat lots of acorns and leaves in fall.

18

Food will be harder to find when winter comes.

How do snowshoe hares change in fall?

CHAPTER 5

READY FOR WINTER

Look! I see the first snowflakes.

Fall is over.
Winter is here.
The animals are ready.

LEARN ABOUT FALL

Gray whales have their babies near Mexico. The waters there are safe and warm.

Monarch butterflies migrate as far as 3,000 miles (4,800 km).

Black bears gain as much as 30 pounds (14 kg) each week in fall. They will not eat in winter.

Young rattlesnakes are born in fall. Sometimes they do not eat until spring.

White-tailed deer grow thicker fur in fall. The fur keeps them warm.

THINK ABOUT FALL:
CRITICAL-THINKING AND TEXT FEATURE QUESTIONS

How can you tell when
it is fall?

Can you think of any other
animals that might migrate
or hibernate in fall?

Can you find the glossary
in this book?

Why are there foxes
in the pictures on
pages 16 and 17?

LERNER

SOURCE

Expand learning beyond the printed book. Download free, complementary
educational resources for this book from our website, www.lerneresource.com.

GLOSSARY

den: a home for a wild animal, such as a bear or a rattlesnake

hibernate: to spend the winter in a deep sleep

migrate: to move from one area to another in fall or spring

TO LEARN MORE

BOOKS

Gleisner, Jenna Lee. *Animals in Fall.* Mankato, MN: Child's World, 2017. Learn more about how animals get ready for winter.

Schuh, Mari. *I Notice Animals in Fall.* Minneapolis: Lerner Publications, 2017. Read more about the animals that migrate, hibernate, and change in fall.

WEBSITE

Activity Village: Autumn
https://www.activityvillage.co.uk/autumn
Find coloring pages, crafts, and activities about fall animals.

INDEX